THE SOLAR SYSTEM

BY ARNOLD RINGSTAD

Published by The Child's World®
1980 Lookout Drive • Mankato, MN 56003-1705
800-599-READ • www.childsworld.com

Photographs ©: JPL/NASA, cover, 1, 2, 3, 6, 9, 11, 12 (top), 15, 16 (Mercury), 16 (Earth), 17 (Neptune), 20; Withan Tor/Shutterstock Images, 4; JSC/NASA, 8, 16 (Venus); NASA, ESA, A. Simon (GSFC), M.H. Wong (University of California, Berkeley) and the OPAL Team/NASA, 12 (bottom), 16–17 (Saturn); JPL-Caltech/NASA, 14, 17 (Uranus), 22; NASA Goddard/GSFC/NASA, 16 (Sun); JPL/USGS/NASA, 16 (Mars); NASA, ESA, A. Simon (Goddard Space Flight Center), and M.H. Wong (University of California, Berkeley)/NASA, 16–17 (Jupiter); Steve Gribben/JPL/NASA, 18; Goddard/Walt Feimer/NASA, 21

ISBN 9781503844759 (Reinforced Library Binding)
ISBN 9781503846180 (Portable Document Format)
ISBN 9781503847378 (Online Multi-user eBook)
LCCN 2019957950

Printed in the United States of America

About the Author

Arnold Ringstad loves reading about space science and exploration. He lives in Minnesota with his wife and their cat.

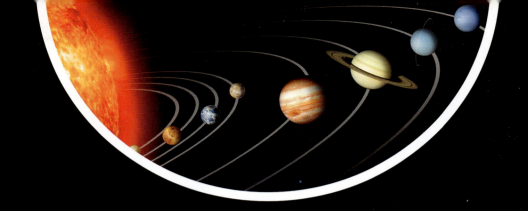

CONTENTS

Sol is the
Latin word
for sun. This
is why the sun and
everything that orbits it is
called the solar system.

CHAPTER ONE

WHAT IS THE SOLAR SYSTEM?

The solar system is made up of the sun and everything that **orbits** it. The sun is a star. It is the largest object in the solar system.

Planets are the biggest objects that orbit the sun. There are eight planets. One of these is Earth. The planets are divided into two groups. There are four inner planets and four outer planets. Earth is one of the inner planets.

The solar system also includes smaller objects called dwarf planets. Finally, it has even smaller objects called asteroids and **comets**. The sun's **gravity** holds all these objects in place.

DID YOU KNOW?

The sun contains 500 times more **mass** than everything else in the solar system put together!

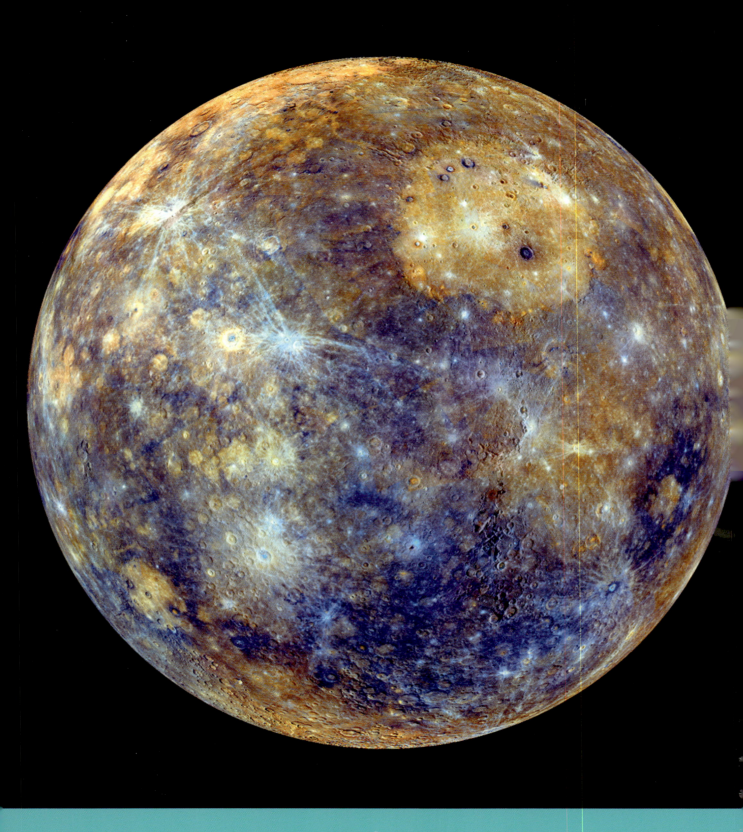

CHAPTER TWO

THE INNER PLANETS

Mercury is the planet closest to the sun. If someone were to stand on Mercury, the sun would look three times bigger than it does from Earth! Mercury is a rocky planet. It has many **craters.** Its surface looks gray or brown. The side of Mercury facing the sun can get very hot. It reaches 800 degrees Fahrenheit (430°C). That's much hotter than an oven!

◄ Mercury is the smallest planet in our solar system.

Venus is the next planet out from the sun. It is about the same size as Earth. But a person wouldn't want to live there. Venus is covered by thick clouds of gas. The gas traps heat near the surface. This makes Venus even hotter than Mercury.

Earth is ▶ our home. Scientists know more about Earth than any other planet.

Earth is the third planet from the sun. It is a colorful world. The land is green and brown. The water is deep blue. Ice and clouds are white. Earth stands out in the solar system. It is the only place where life is known to live.

◀ Venus spins backward compared to Earth. This means on Venus, the sun rises in the west and sets in the east.

The last inner planet is Mars. It has a rusty red color. Mars gets very cold. The **atmosphere** is thin. Someday people may travel to Mars. They could walk on the surface. Many robotic spacecraft have already started exploring the planet.

Beyond Mars is the asteroid belt. This is a group of asteroids that orbit the sun. Asteroids are rocks left over from when the planets formed. Most of the asteroids in the solar system are in the asteroid belt. These asteroids come in many sizes. Some are more than 300 miles (480 km) across. Others are fewer than 33 feet (10 m) across. Scientists know of more than 800,000 asteroids in our solar system.

Humans have not been to Mars yet. But robots called rovers ▶ have sent pictures of Mars's surface back to scientists on Earth.

▲
Jupiter has 79 moons.
A NASA spacecraft
called *Cassini* took this
picture of Jupiter with
Io, one of its moons.

Saturn is not the ▶
only gas giant to
have rings, but its rings
are the most visible.

CHAPTER THREE

THE OUTER PLANETS

The first outer planet is Jupiter. It is the solar system's largest planet. It has more than twice as much mass as all the other planets put together. Jupiter is a gas giant. That means it is made up of swirling gases. There is no hard ground to stand on. Huge storms blow across the planet. One of these storms is even bigger than Earth.

Saturn is the next planet out from the sun. It is a gas giant, too. Saturn is famous for its beautiful rings. These rings are made up of chunks of ice and rock. Some of these chunks are the size of dust grains. Others are as big as buildings.

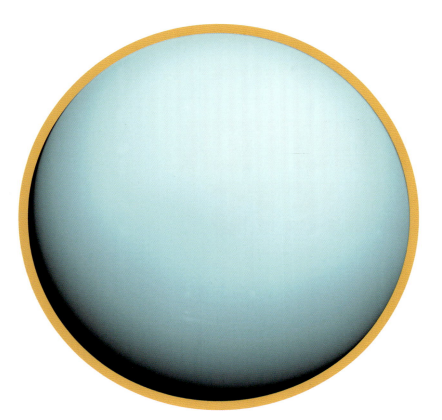

◀ Uranus rotates on its side. *Voyager 2* is the only spacecraft to fly by Uranus. It took this picture in 1986.

The seventh planet from the sun is Uranus. It is smaller than Jupiter and Saturn, but it is still huge. It is about four times wider than Earth. Uranus is known as an ice giant. It is made up of swirling icy materials. One of these is called methane. Earth has methane, too. But Uranus has more of it, and the methane is much colder. The methane gives the planet its light blue color.

According to NASA, Neptune is the windiest planet. ▶

The final known planet in the solar system is Neptune. It is similar to Uranus in size, but it is much farther from the sun. Like Uranus, Neptune is an ice giant. It is made of similar icy materials and also has a blue color.

DID YOU KNOW?

The outer planets have many moons. Neptune has 14 and Uranus has 27. Jupiter has 79 of them. Saturn has the most, with an amazing 82 moons!

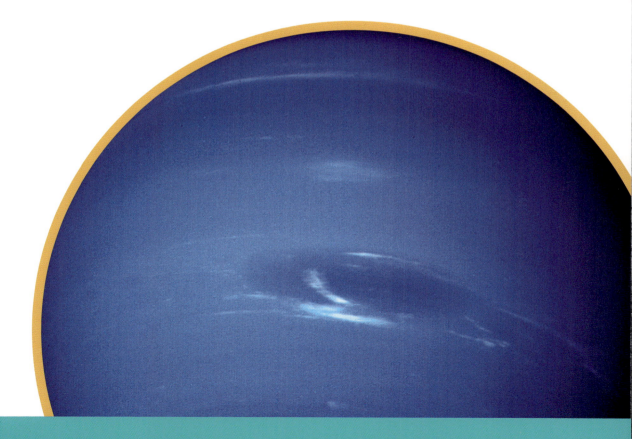

Sizes of Planets in our Solar System

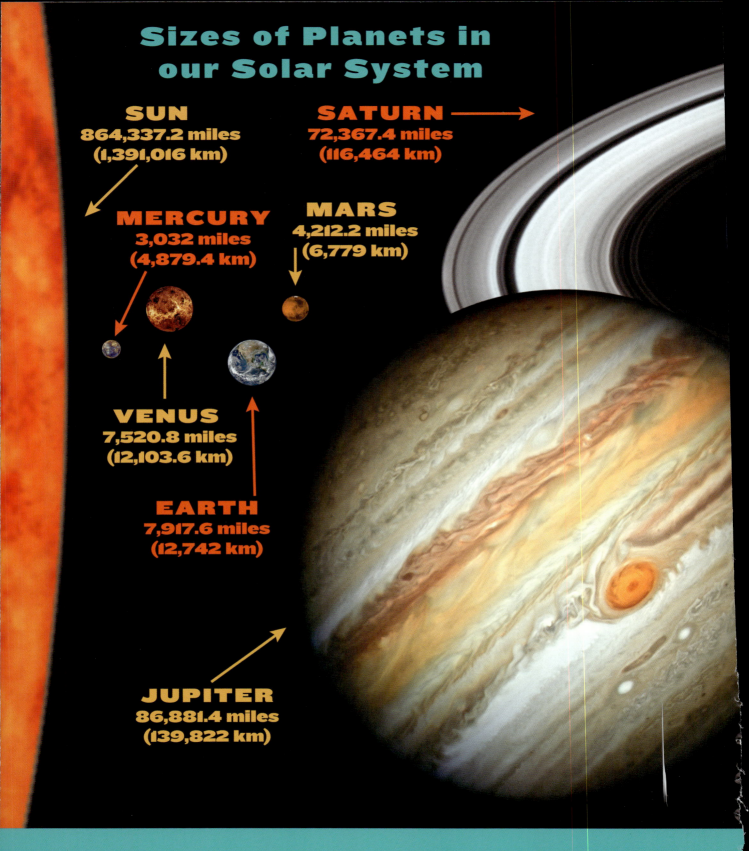

SUN
864,337.2 miles
(1,391,016 km)

SATURN →

72,367.4 miles
(116,464 km)

MERCURY
3,032 miles
(4,879.4 km)

MARS
4,212.2 miles
(6,779 km)

VENUS
7,520.8 miles
(12,103.6 km)

EARTH
7,917.6 miles
(12,742 km)

JUPITER
86,881.4 miles
(139,822 km)

NEPTUNE
30,598.8 miles
(49,244 km)

URANUS
31,518.4 miles
(50,724 km)

The size given is the width across the planet. Planets are shown with size to scale. The distance between planets is not to scale.

CHAPTER FOUR

THE SOLAR SYSTEM'S EDGE

The solar system contains even more objects and areas beyond Neptune. One area is called the Kuiper (KY-pur) Belt. It is named for astronomer Gerard Kuiper. The Kuiper Belt contains millions of small, icy objects. It is shaped like a gigantic donut circling the solar system. Some Kuiper Belt objects are comets. These are made of rock, ice, and dust. They sometimes travel to the inner solar system.

◄ The Kuiper Belt lies past Neptune. This is an artist's illustration of an object in the Kuiper Belt.

Beyond the Kuiper Belt is the **heliopause**. This is the distance where the **solar wind** is balanced by pressure from outside the solar system. The solar system has no clear edge. But when a spacecraft reaches this point, scientists sometimes say it has left the solar system.

Still, there is an even more distant area. It is called the Oort cloud. It is shaped like a huge bubble around the solar system. The icy objects there are as big as mountains. Many comets come from the Oort cloud.

Past the Oort cloud is a wide area of empty space. Very far away, there are other stars with their own solar systems. Our own solar system is just one of millions of solar systems in our galaxy.

OUTSIDE PRESSURE

SOLAR WIND

HELIOPAUSE

▲
The heliopause occurs where pressure from solar wind is
the same as pressure from outside the solar system.

DID YOU KNOW?

The largest object in the Kuiper Belt used to be a
planet. Pluto was once seen as the ninth planet.
Now it is called a dwarf planet.

VOYAGE TO THE OUTER SOLAR SYSTEM

In the 1970s, the outer planets were lined up in a special way. A spacecraft would be able to visit all four of them. The United States created the Voyager program to carry out this mission. It launched *Voyager 1* and *Voyager 2* in 1977.

The spacecraft both reached Jupiter in 1979. Then they split up. *Voyager 1* took one path to Saturn in 1980. Then it flew past Titan, one of Saturn's moons. After that, its mission was done. *Voyager 2* took another path to Saturn. It got there in 1981. Then it kept going. The spacecraft flew past Uranus in 1986 and Neptune in 1989. In 2018, it passed through the heliopause.

The Voyager program was a big success. The spacecraft took amazing photos. They collected important scientific data. They helped scientists learn a lot about the outer solar system.

Voyager 2 launched in 1977 from the Kennedy Space Center in Cape Canaveral, Florida.

GLOSSARY

atmosphere (AT-muss-feer) An atmosphere is the layer of gases that surrounds a planet. Mars has a thin atmosphere.

comets (KAH-mitz) Comets are chunks of rock and ice that orbit the sun. Many comets come from the Oort cloud.

craters (KRAY-turz) Craters are large holes dug in the ground when rocks from space slam into a moon, planet, or dwarf planet. Mercury is covered in craters.

gravity (GRAV-i-tee) Gravity is the force that pulls objects together. The sun's gravity holds the solar system together.

heliopause (HEE-lee-oh-paws) The heliopause is the area in space where the solar wind balances with pressure coming from outside the solar system. *Voyager 2* passed through the heliopause in 2018.

mass (MASS) Mass is a measure of how much matter is in an object. The sun makes up most of the mass in the solar system.

orbits (OR-bits) An object orbits the sun when it travels in a round path around the sun. When Earth orbits the sun, it takes one year to go around.

solar wind (SOH-ler WIND) The solar wind is a stream of particles coming from the sun. The solar wind balances with pressure outside the solar system at the heliopause.

TO LEARN MORE

IN THE LIBRARY

Rathburn, Betsy. *Planets*. Minneapolis, MN:
Bellwether Media, 2019.

Sabol, Stephanie. *Where Is Our Solar System?*
New York, NY: Penguin Workshop, 2018.

Solar System. New York, NY: DK Publishing, 2016.

ON THE WEB

Visit our website for links about the solar system:

childsworld.com/links

*Note to Parents, Teachers, and Librarians: We routinely verify
our Web links to make sure they are safe and active sites.
So encourage your readers to check them out!*

INDEX